NIGHT DRIVING

JOHN COY

ILLUSTRATED BY
PETER McCARTY

HENRY HOLT AND COMPANY

NEW YORK

Henry Holt and Company, LLC
Publishers since 1866
115 West 18th Street
New York, New York 10011
www.henryholt.com

Library of Congress Cataloging-in-Publication Data
Coy, John.
Night driving / by John Coy; illustrated by Peter McCarty.
Summary: As father and son drive into the night,
they watch the sunset, talk about baseball, sing cowboy songs,
and even change a flat tire before pitching camp at daybreak.
[1. Fathers and sons—Fiction. 2. Night—Fiction. 3. Travel—Fiction.]
I. McCarty, Peter ill. II. Title.
PZ7.C839455Ni 1995 [E]—dc20 95-6063

ISBN 0-8050-2931-1 (hardcover)
5 7 9 10 8 6 4
ISBN 0-8050-6708-6 (paperback)
3 5 7 9 10 8 6 4 2

First published in hardcover in 1996 by Henry Holt and Company
First Owlet paperback edition—2001
The artist used pencil on paper to create the illustrations for this book.
Manufactured in China

For everyone driving in the night
—J. C.

For my dad
—P. McC.

My dad and I are driving west.

We started this afternoon, and I'm excited because it's my first trip to the mountains and we're going to sleep in a tent.

Ahead, the sun sets in a mix of orange and pink.

"Are we almost there?"

"Oh no, it's a long way. We'll do some night driving."

"Why are we going to drive at night?"

"It's cooler when the sun is down and we have the road to ourselves. We should see mountains by morning."

Dad turns on the radio and finds a game.

"Listening to baseball helps eat up the miles."

I imagine the car as a giant mouth gobbling up the road.

"Look, there in the ditch." Dad hits the brakes, and two pairs of eyes shine. "Those are mule deer."

I watch the deer leap a fence and bound into a field.

"Many animals come out at night," Dad says. "Keep your eyes open."

As we drive, Dad unscrews the cap of his thermos.

"Can you take the wheel?"

"Sure."

I watch the lines and steer straight while Dad pours coffee.

Steam rises from the cup. I like the smell of coffee, but the taste is too strong.

As he looks ahead, my dad tells stories about when he was a boy. I look at his face and imagine what he was like.

Behind him, the sky is black. In front of us, it's purple.

"These summer sunsets on the prairie seem to last forever."

"How late can I stay up?"

"As late as you want."

Behind us, like a giant's night light, the full moon has risen.

"That moon is so bright," Dad says. "We could drive without headlights."

"Really?"

"Sure. No cars on a straight road. This is a good spot."

He slows down, then clicks off the lights.

"Wow!" The road glows in the moonlight.

Dad turns the lights back on.

"I could still see."

"Yes," he says. "Same moon, but out here, it's so much brighter."

Kaflump, kaflump . . .

"What's that?"

"Sounds like a flat," Dad tightens his hands on the wheel as the car bumps to a stop.

"Will we still make it to the mountains?"

"Oh yeah. You can help change it."

I hold the flashlight as my dad gets tools from the trunk. He presses the jack and the car lifts off the ground. I hand him wheel nuts, and when the spare tire is on, he lets the car down.

After he puts the tools away, Dad stretches and rolls his head.

"There's the Big Dipper."

He shows me how to draw a line from two stars in the Dipper to Polaris, the North Star.

The sky here is huge, and a chorus of crickets chirps. I pick up a smooth rock.

"Watch my fastball."

I throw as hard as I can, and the rock sails into the dark.

Back in the car, the game on the radio has faded, so I switch to western music. Dad teaches me cowboy songs, and we sing together.

A semi passes us with its lights glowing. Dad flashes the headlights so the trucker knows it's safe to pull back in. The trucker flashes back to say thanks.

We stop at a gas station in a small town.

While my dad gets the tire fixed, I help the attendant. He lets me pump gas while he washes the windows.

My dad comes over holding a sharp piece of metal.

"This was in the tire."

He fills his thermos at the cafe next door, and we each get a doughnut. As we leave town, two juicy bugs splat against the clean windshield.

"Let's play the letter game."

"A is ashtray," my dad starts.

 I watch until we cross a dry creek gulch.

"B is bridge."

 At Y, Dad points to his mouth and yawns.

 I look over at the green glow of the speedometer.

"And Z is zero."

 It's cooler now. I reach in back for my blue jacket and put it on.

"Do you want to rest awhile?" Dad asks.

"Oh no, I'm not tired one bit."

No stations come in clearly, so Dad turns off the radio. He sips coffee and tells me stories about growing up. He tells me about his dad, who died when I was little.

"Your grandpa was left-handed and a fine pitcher. He might have played in the big leagues, but he hurt his arm one summer when he threw too much. He always loved baseball."

"I love baseball."

"He would have liked knowing you."

My dad stops talking, and I know he's thinking about his dad. I wish my grandpa was still here. We drive awhile in silence, and I listen to the hum of the engine.

We stop at a wayside rest where the outhouse smells bad. Inside, it's dark and flies buzz. I hold my breath, hurry to finish, then rush outside.

My dad laughs. "Let's go down to the water."

As we walk, a cloud crosses the moon.

"Use your night vision, and let your eyes adjust to the dark."

At the river, I put my hands in.

"That water's cold."

"It's from snow in the mountains."

My dad bends down, cups water and splashes his face.

I do too. The cool air on my wet face feels good. We squat together and listen to the gurgling water.

As we walk to the car, I look up at a million stars and find Polaris.

Now we play an alphabet game of people. A is Abraham Lincoln. B is Babe Ruth. My dad tells stories about each person, so this game lasts a long time.

There are no other cars out now, and we've been driving for hours. I hear the *thp, thp, thp* of tires rolling over cracks in the road and wonder if I'll stay awake.

I look over at my dad's heavy eyes.

"Are you getting tired?"

"Yes," he says. "We need a break."

Ahead, orange letters flash EAT.

"Stopping for breakfast," Dad says, "is my favorite part of driving at night."

Inside, people are talking and eating. A cowboy is singing to the jukebox.

"You sing as bad as you tip," says the waitress.

"Worse," says the cook, and everyone laughs.

The waitress is surprised when she comes to our booth.

"You're up early."

"Late," I say. "We've been night driving and I stayed up the whole time."

When the food comes, the pancakes are so big they cover the plate.

"Night driving makes me really hungry," I tell my dad.

"Me too," he says, and we both smile.

After we eat, Dad reads the paper and drinks more coffee. Behind him, the sky is lighter.

When Dad finishes, we walk outside. Suddenly, I see giant peaks, sharp as bear's teeth, that push into the sky.

"Look, Dad, the mountains."

I feel his hand on my shoulder, and way up high, I see snow sparkling in the light.

"We made it," I say. "Let's go set up the tent."